The Tale of Peter Rabbit

By Beatrix Potter

Illustrated by Ann Schweninger

A GOLDEN BOOK • NEW YORK

Western Publishing Company, Inc., Racine, Wisconsin 53404

Once upon a time there were four little Rabbits, and their names were—Flopsy, Mopsy, Cottontail, and Peter. They lived with their mother in a sandbank, underneath the root of a very big fir tree.

"Now, my dears," said old Mrs. Rabbit one morning, "you may go into the fields or down the lane, but don't go into Mr. McGregor's garden. Your father had an accident there. He was put in a pie by Mrs. McGregor. Now run along and don't get into mischief. I am going out."

Then old Mrs. Rabbit took a basket and her umbrella and went through the wood to the baker's. She bought a loaf of brown bread and five currant buns.

Flopsy, Mopsy, and Cottontail, who were good little bunnies, went down the lane to gather blackberries. But Peter, who was very naughty, ran straight away to Mr. McGregor's garden and squeezed under the gate!

First he ate some lettuces
and some French beans . . .

and then he ate
some radishes.

And then, feeling
rather sick, he went
to look for some parsley.

But round the end of a cucumber frame, whom should he meet but Mr. McGregor! Mr. McGregor was on his hands and knees planting out young cabbages, but he jumped up and ran after Peter, waving a rake and calling out, "Stop, thief!"

Peter was most dreadfully frightened. He rushed all over the garden, for he had forgotten the way back to the gate.

He lost one of his shoes among the cabbages, and the other shoe among the potatoes. After losing them, he ran on four legs and went faster, so that he might have got away altogether if . . .

he had not unfortunately run into a gooseberry net and got caught by the large buttons on his jacket. It was a blue jacket with brass buttons, quite new.

Peter gave himself up for lost and shed big tears. But his sobs were overheard by some friendly sparrows, who flew to him in great excitement, and implored him to exert himself.

Mr. McGregor came up with a sieve, which he intended to pop upon the top of Peter. But Peter wriggled out just in time, leaving his jacket behind, and rushed into the tool shed . . .

and jumped into a can. It would have been a beautiful thing to hide in if it had not had so much water in it.

Mr. McGregor was quite sure that Peter was somewhere in the tool shed, perhaps hidden underneath a flowerpot. He began to turn them over carefully, looking under each.

Presently Peter sneezed—*kertyshoo*! Mr. McGregor was after him in no time and tried to put his foot upon Peter, who jumped out of a window, upsetting three plants. Mr. McGregor was tired of running after Peter. He went back to his work.

Peter sat down to rest. He was out of breath and
trembling with fright, and he had not the least idea
which way to go.

After a time he began to wander about, going
lippity-lippity—not very fast and looking all around.

He found a door in a wall, but it was locked, and
there was no room for a fat little rabbit to squeeze
underneath.

An old mouse was running in and out over the stone doorstep, carrying peas and beans to her family in the wood. Peter asked her the way to the gate, but she had such a large pea in her mouth that she could not answer. She only shook her head at him. Peter began to cry.

Then he tried to find his way straight across the garden, but he became more and more puzzled. Presently he came to a pond where Mr. McGregor filled his water cans.

A white cat was staring at some goldfish. She sat
very, very still, but now and then the tip of her tail
twitched as if it were alive. Peter thought it best to go
away without speaking to her. He had heard about cats
from his cousin, little Benjamin Bunny.

He went back towards the tool shed, but suddenly quite close to him, he heard the noise of a hoe—*scr-r-ritch, scratch, scratch, scritch*. Peter scuttered underneath the bushes.

But presently, as nothing happened, he came out and climbed upon a wheelbarrow and peeped over. The first thing he saw was Mr. McGregor hoeing onions. His back was turned towards Peter, and beyond him was the gate!

Peter got down very quietly off the wheelbarrow and started running as fast as he could go along a straight walk behind some black currant bushes.

Mr. McGregor caught sight of him at the corner, but Peter did not care. He slipped underneath the gate and was safe at last in the wood outside the garden.

Mr. McGregor hung up the little jacket and the shoes for a scarecrow to frighten the blackbirds.

Peter never stopped running and never looked behind him till he got home to the big fir tree.

He was so tired that he flopped down upon the nice soft sand on the floor of the rabbit hole and shut his eyes. His mother was busy cooking. She wondered what he had done with his clothes. It was the second little jacket and pair of shoes that Peter had lost in a fortnight!

I am sorry to say that Peter was not very well during the evening.

His mother put him to bed and made some camomile tea. And she gave a dose of it to Peter!

"One tablespoonful to be taken at bedtime."

But Flopsy, Mopsy, and Cottontail had bread and milk and blackberries for supper.